Terry Jones

The Fly-by-Night

Illustrated by
Michael Foreman

PUFFIN BOOKS

Some other books by Terry Jones and Michael Foreman

Picture books

THE BEAST WITH A THOUSAND TEETH
A FISH OF THE WORLD
THE SEA TIGER

Fiction

FAIRY TALES
FANTASTIC STORIES
NICOBOBINUS
THE SAGA OF ERIK THE VIKING

Some other books by Terry Jones

Poetry

THE CURSE OF THE VAMPIRE'S SOCKS

Penguin Children's 60s

THE DRAGON ON THE ROOF

Some other books by Michael Foreman

Picture books

DINOSAURS AND ALL THAT RUBBISH
LONG NECK AND THUNDER FOOT
(with Helen Piers)
THE SELFISH GIANT
(with Oscar Wilde and Freire Wright)
TEENY-TINY AND THE WITCH-WOMAN
(with Barbara Walker)
THERE'S A BEAR IN THE BATH
(with Nanette Newman)
WAR AND PEAS

Fiction

LAND OF THE LONG WHITE CLOUD
(with Kiri Te Kanawa)

Non-fiction

AFTER THE WAR WAS OVER
WAR BOY: A COUNTRY CHILDHOOD
WAR GAME

PUFFIN BOOKS

Published by the Penguin Group
Penguin Books Ltd, 27 Wrights Lane, London W8 5TZ, England
Penguin Books USA Inc., 375 Hudson Street, New York, New York 10014, USA
Penguin Books Australia Ltd, Ringwood, Victoria, Australia
Penguin Books Canada Ltd, 10 Alcorn Avenue, Toronto, Ontario, Canada M4V 3B2
Penguin Books (NZ) Ltd, 182–190 Wairau Road, Auckland 10, New Zealand

Penguin Books Ltd, Registered Offices: Harmondsworth, Middlesex, England

First published by Pavilion Books Limited 1994
Published in Puffin Books 1997
1 3 5 7 9 10 8 6 4 2

Designed by Bet Ayer

Printed in Hong Kong by Imago Publishing Limited

little girl was lying in bed one night
when she heard a tapping on her
window. She was rather frightened, but
she went to the window and opened it, telling
herself that it was probably just the wind. But when
she looked out, do you know what she saw?
It was a little creature as black as soot with bright
yellow eyes, and it was sitting on a cat that appeared
to be flying.

'Hello,' said the creature, 'would you like to come flying?'

'Yes, *please!*' said the little girl, and she climbed out of the window on to the cat and off they flew.

'Hang on tight!' cried the creature.

'Where are we going?' asked the little girl.

'I don't know!' called the creature.

'Who are you?' asked the little girl.

'I haven't got a name,' said the creature, 'I'm just a fly-by-night!' And up they went into the air, over the hills and away.

The little girl looked around her at the bright moon
and the stars that seemed to wink at her and chuckle to
themselves. Then she looked down at the black world
below her, and she was suddenly frightened again, and
said: 'How will we find our way back?'

'Oh! Don't worry about *that*!' cried the fly-by-night.
'What does it matter?' And he leant on the cat's whiskers
and down they swooped towards the dark earth.

'But I must be able to get home!' cried the little girl. 'My mother and father will wonder where I am!'

'Oh! Poop-de-doo!' cried the fly-by-night, and he pulled back on the cat's whiskers and up they soared – up and up into the stars again, and all the stars were humming in rhythm:

> Boodle-dum-dee
> Boodle-dum-da,
> Isn't it great,
> Being a star!

And all the stars had hands, and they started clapping together in unison. Then suddenly the moon opened his mouth and sang in a loud booming voice:

> I'm just the moon,
> But that's fine by me
> As long as I hear that
> Boodle-dum-dee!

And the cat opened its mouth wide and sang:
'Wheeeeeeee!' and they looped-the-loop and turned
circles to the rhythm of the stars.

But the little girl started to cry and said: 'Oh please, I
want to go home!'

'Oh no you don't!' cried the fly-by-night, and took
the cat straight up as fast as they could go, and the stars
seemed to flash past them like silver darts.

'Please!' cried the little girl. 'Take me back!'

'Spoilsport!' yelled the fly-by-night and he stopped the cat dead, then tipped it over, and down they swooped so fast that they left their stomachs behind them at the top, and landed on a silent hill.

'Here you are!' said the fly-by-night.

'But this isn't my home,' said the little girl, looking around at the dark, lonely countryside.

'Oh! It'll be around somewhere, I expect,' said the fly-by-night.

'But we've come miles and miles from my home!' cried the little girl.

But it was too late. The fly-by-night had pulled back on the cat's whiskers and away he soared up into the night sky, and the last the little girl saw of him was a black shape silhouetted against the moon.

The little girl shivered and looked around her, wondering if there were any wild animals about.

'Which way should I go?' she wondered.

'Try the path through the wood,' said a stone at her feet. So she set off along the path that led through the dark wood.

As soon as she got amongst the trees, the leaves
blotted out the light of the moon, branches clutched at
her hair, and roots tried to trip up her feet, and she
thought she heard the trees snigger, quietly; and they
seemed to say to each other: 'That'll teach her to go off
with a fly-by-night!'

Suddenly she felt a cold hand gripping her neck, but
it was just a cobweb strung with dew. And she heard
the spider busy itself with repairs, muttering: 'Tut-tut-
tut-tut. She went off with a fly-by-night! Tut-tut-tut-tut.'

As the little girl peered into the wood, she thought she could see eyes watching her and winking to each other and little voices you couldn't really hear whispered under the broad leaves: 'What a silly girl – to go off with a fly-by-night! She should have known better! Tut-tut-tut-tut.'

Eventually she felt so miserable and so foolish that
she just sat down and cried by a still pond.

'Now then, what's the matter?' said a kindly voice.

The little girl looked up, and then all around her, but
she couldn't see anyone.

'Who's that?' she asked.

'Look in the pond,' said the voice, and she looked down and saw the reflection of the moon, smiling up at her out of the pond.

'Don't take on so,' said the moon.

'But I've been so silly,' said the little girl, 'and now I'm quite, quite lost and I don't know how I'll *ever* get home.'

'You'll get home all right,' said the moon's reflection. 'Hop on a lily-pad and follow me.'

So the little girl stepped cautiously on to a lily-pad, and the moon's reflection started to move slowly across the pond and then down a stream, and the little girl paddled the lily-pad after it.

Slowly and silently they slipped through the night
forest, and then out into the open fields, where they
followed the stream until they came to a hill she
recognized, and suddenly there was her own house.

She ran as fast as she could and climbed in through the window of her own room and snuggled into her own dear bed.

And the moon smiled in at her through the window, and she fell asleep thinking how silly she'd been to go off with the fly-by-night. But, you know, somewhere, deep down inside her, she half hoped she'd hear another tap on her window one day and find another fly-by-night offering her a ride on its flying cat.

But she never did.